Amish Pen Pals

Rachael's Confession

Karen Anna Vogel

With Dr. Maryann Roberts

Lamb Books

Amish Pen Pals: Rachael's Confession

Contact the author on Facebook at: www.facebook.com/VogelReaders

Learn more the author at: www.karenannavogel.com

Visit her blog, Amish Crossings, at www.karenannavogel.blogspot.com

DEDICATION

To faithful readers worldwide who feel that the fictitious Granny Weaver in my *Amish Knitting Circle Series* is their very own grandmother, giving them sage advice. Your encouragement fuels me to continue writing about her, keeping Granny alive.

Danki

Table of Contents

INTRODUCTION

Dear Friends,

I receive letters asking for advice after reading one of my *Amish Knitting Circle Series* books. If they had friendships like the women in the circle, what guidance would they give concerning their issues?

Many also contact me to see if I can hook them up with an Amish pen pal to get personal one-on-one advice. Although many Amish do have non-Amish pen pals, I don't know of a way to make the connection. I tell readers to visit an Amish settlement and make an initial contact by asking for a recipe. Amish women love to share their recipes! This is a good way to make an Amish friend, and then perhaps, you can write to each other.

Amish Pen Pals will be a series of complete novellas, each tackling a problem and the counsel an Amish pen pal would give, consistent with their view on Christian living. I've asked Dr. Maryann Roberts, a gifted Christian counselor and friend, to make a discussion guide so you can dig deeper or use for personal reflection after you finish the story.

If there's a problem you'd like to see addressed in this series, please contact me at www.karenannavogel.com

I hope you are blessed by this series.

Karen Anna Vogel

Amish – English Dictionary

Pennsylvania Dutch dialect is used throughout this book, common to the Amish of Western Pennsylvania. You may want to refer to this little dictionary from time to time.

Ach – Oh
Daed – Dad
Dawdyhaus – Small house built for grandparents near the main farmhouse
Dochder – Daughter
English (Englisher) - What the Amish call those outside their faith.
Eck table –Special table set in the corner for the bridal party
Gmay – community; a church district, usually made up of two-hundred people
Goot – Good
Grandkinner – Grandchildren
Ya – Yes
Kapp – Prayer cap used by Amish women to cover their head
Kinner – Children
Mamm – Mom
Nee – No
Old Christmas – January 6th, commemorating the coming of the Magi, ending the Twelve Days of Christmas.
Rumspringa - a period of adolescence in which boys and girls are given greater personal freedom and allowed to form romantic relationships, usually ending with the choice of baptism into the church or leaving the community. (Oxford Dictionary)
Second Christmas –The Amish celebrate Christmas on the 25th like the English, but have a second celebration the next day.
Yinz – Plural form of you, common to Western Pennsylvania Amish and English.

CHAPTER 1

A Burden

Rachael stared at the bare tree limbs casting shadows over the vast field of withered brown cornstalks and groaned. From her bedroom in her parent's massive two story farmhouse, she breathed a prayer for peace. The sin buried deep inside was heavy and her morning ritual was to beg for it to be lifted.

She pulled the black shawl she'd made over her shoulders and shivered. How could she have been so naïve? So vulnerable? As was her daily morning exercise, she got down on her knees and begged God to blot out her sin… and that it never be found out.

Rachael quickly picked one of the five dresses she had off the pegboard, and then she brushed her hair one-hundred strokes and pulled it into a massive blond ponytail at the nape of her neck. *He ran his fingers through my hair*, she caught herself remembering, and shook her head to get the memory to dislodge. When would this mental torment end? She pinned her hair up in her usual flat way around the back of her head and put on a black *kapp*.

A rhythmic tap on her bedroom door told her that breakfast needed to be made. Eli, her older brother by two years, was done with farm chores, being up since four a.m., and was famished, but he had a skip in his step, most likely excited to announce his engagement in a few days. The November wedding season only made Rachael's heart sink lower. She would never be married. No, she did not deserve a good Amish man. Not somebody like Samuel Miller, even though his big hazel eyes pled for understanding…

Rachael sauntered downstairs and opening the woodstove door, was relieved that Eli had started a fire. The chilly first floor prompted Rachael to move about the kitchen, her place of solace.

"*Goot* morning, Rachael," her *mamm* said as she rounded the corner, coming out of the utility room off the kitchen. "Cold day to hang laundry…"

"But more hands make less work."

Mattie's light blue eyes crinkled at the sides as she smiled. "Ach, to have a dochder like you, so willing to help. You'll make a *goot* wife."

Rachael spun around to get flour out of the pantry to make cinnamon flop for breakfast, avoiding eye contact with her *mamm*.

"I see how Samuel looks at you. Will there be an announcement soon? Will you and Eli be wed on the same day?" Mattie clasped her hands. "This big old farmhouse will be full of guests."

Rachael measured flour into a bowl. "Eli will wed at Sadie's house, I'm thinking. As for me, there will be no announcement. I'm content to teach."

Mattie went over to Rachael and gently put her slender fingers on her shoulders, turning her around. "You feel content today to teach because we take each day as they come. When you wed, you will feel content, too."

Rachael tried to hide her emotions, buried deep.

Mattie touched Rachael's cheek. "Why do your eyes darken whenever I speak of marriage? Is it your sister?"

Rachael shrugged her shoulders. An ache like no other welled within her, but she stifled any emotion.

"Ach, there are days I pine for my Kate," Mattie confided. "And if I'd only warned her not to go out…"

"*Mamm*, please, don't blame yourself."

"I should have not been so outspoken. Your *daed* didn't want her to deliver the quilt but I was too worried about money. My greed…" Mattie ambled over to the coffee pot that lived on the stove, ready to heat a body on a chilly day.

"*Mamm*, money's tight and you're like the woman in Proverbs, making items to sell at the market." Rachael went to her *mamm* and slipped an arm around her. "You're the best *mamm* anyone could ask for… and friend. It wasn't your fault."

A tear slipped down Mattie's cheek and she embraced Rachael. "I feel the same about you. A *dochder* and friend. And I'm selfish to dwell on myself when you must miss Kate something awful."

Rachael squeezed her *mamm* tight, but knowing her *daed* and brother would be looking to eat by seven, she resumed baking, rolling out the dough into circles. "I miss Kate at nights as the room is so empty without her. They say twins have a bond like no other siblings."

Mattie forced a smile. "*Yinz* girls could have had any of the bedrooms in the house with the other *kinner* married and gone, but shared a room. I'd say that's a special bond." She cracked eggs and beat them in a bowl. "I heard you talking late into the night."

"I told Kate everything. Maybe too much." The night before her sister's death, the beans she'd spilt had stunned her sister and most likely the reason why she needed to get away the next morning. Did she drive past the hill overlooking Troutville to see something of beauty after all the ugliness that she'd heard from Rachael's lips?

Did she stop to see the *"houses dotting the autumn foliage, their chimneys breathing out gray smoke"*, as she described the scene a few days before the accident? How enthusiastic she was to sketch the view to make it into an applique quilt.

Rachael chided herself once again. *It was her fault that her sister died.* If only she could tell her *mamm* the truth…

"Well," Mattie broke the quiet, "you have a *goot* friend in Samuel. Look at the gifts he brings. That compliment box was real nice."

Rachael felt her heart twist in pain. *"Ya,* it was thoughtful."

"And you know Jebediah Weaver, his pen pal down in Smicksburg, gave him that idea. He and Deborah seem to be able to help so many young folk." Mattie dispensed the eggs into the skillet. "Maybe Deborah Weaver could help you."

"Help me with what?"

"Rachael, we all feel the sting of death sometimes, even though the scriptures tell us God took the sting out of it."

Rachel stopped rolling the dough out on the countertop and put a hand on her *mamm's* shoulder. "We need more time. It's only been a year."

"Kate would want you to move on. To marry Samuel…"

Rachael poked holes with her fingers into the dough, making dents that would fill with a cinnamon, sugar and butter mixture. *Holes.* Her heart was a hole filled with guilt and sorrow over something else, too. But how could her *mamm* understand that?

"I think we should visit Deborah, or Granny, as her girls call her."

"Her girls?"

"The girls in her knitting circle. They meet at her house once a week and knit for charity. But the girls open up, telling Granny and the others their burdens, and they help carry them. The stories she tells in her letters, always written on beautiful floral stationery, usually with red roses..."

"I see them on the table at times. Why such fancy stationery?"

"Jeb planted a rose bush thirty-some years ago when they lost a *dochder.*" Mattie gazed emotionless out the kitchen window. "She misses her roses in the winter, I'm thinking." Mattie's voice faltered as she continued to stare out the window.

"*Mamm*, did the rosebush help?"

"Not at first, but time heals, Granny said. She has climbing roses all around her porch now. Jeb has a green thumb and gets clippings from the plants, helping them take root in mason jars.

But sometimes he surprises her with a new heirloom rose bush." Mattie turned and flipped the eggs onto a platter. "I sure would like to visit her."

Rachael had prayed this morning for the weight to somehow be lifted off her heart. And her dear *mamm* needed support, too. *But could Granny help? Could anyone?* "So, you say Granny helps young people. You mean teenagers?"

"*Nee*, women of all ages, and not just Amish, either. She makes pies for homeless *mamms* the Baptist church helps."

"Homeless *mamms*? Where're the husbands?"

"They don't have husbands," Mattie said under her breath. "*Ya*, Granny seems to accept all kinds of people that many would not associate with."

The tone in her *mamm's* voice reinforced her decision never to tell her about her sin. But this Granny seemed like a rarity, helping all kinds of people that many would not associate with. Rachael poured the cinnamon mixture over the dough, watching it fill the little dents. Could Granny help her?

~*~

As the wind whipped against his cheeks, Samuel Miller wished he was married so he could wear a beard. But he had to remain clean-shaven, letting everyone know he was single and available. But he wasn't. His heart belonged to Rachael, even though she protested, saying she was called to be a teacher. But the way she looked at him at times gave him the impression that she cared.

He lifted a good sized log and set it on their chopping block; a tree stump that once held upright a large maple tree that had provided so much maple syrup, much to his *mamm's* delight. But the ice storm a year back had claimed its life, snapping branches off one by one, a long death.

He swung the ax and split the log in two. The image of Kate Yoder's funeral blew into his mind. The ice had killed more than trees. He'd tried to console Rachael, but she avoided any comfort by anyone, as if it annoyed her.

He turned one piece of the log that lay on the white frost-tipped ground, and cracked it in two. Taking another log from the cord of wood that lay in perfect rows under the shed that sheltered it, he continued to split log after log, all the while pondering Rachael's behavior.

Now that he had his own taxidermy shop on his parent's property, he was set to take a bride, along with the forty acres his parents gave him to farm. Why did Rachael say no to marriage? The girl's blue eyes that once held pure sunlight were now shadowed. Her rosy cheeks were sallow and dark circles underscored her eyes. But to Samuel, she was still a beauty and he would wait. Wait on God and trust.

Delight yourself in the Lord and he will give you the desires of your heart, he'd read today in his daily devotions. He desired to be wed to Rachael, having known her since grade school. When she started to court Zeke for a few short months last year, Samuel was ready to give up altogether, but he had a way of seeing through Rachael, and he believed she never cared for Zeke. This love he had for Rachael must be divine, being so pure and patient. And like his old pen pal Jeb Weaver said, God doesn't lead us down dead-end roads.

As Samuel continued to chop, sweat formed on his face, so he took off his jacket and sat on the bench near the woodpile. Jeb Weaver was married to a spunky woman, as he put it. A woman with a mind of her own, and he admired her for it. Maybe that's what made him attracted to Rachael, but how could he win her heart? The compliment box didn't seem to be working. He'd carved it himself, at Jeb's suggestion, even got brass hinges and stained it cherry. He filled it with all his loving thoughts towards her, all he admired, but she was as cold towards him as a February morning. If Rachael hadn't been the carefree, happy teenager Samuel had known so well, and if his memory wasn't so good, remembering the 'old Rachael', he'd give up or think her a real snob. But he remembered too many summer days, picking berries, helping her with her gardening, even volunteering at her vegetable stand…

CHAPTER 2

~~~~~~~

A Helper

D*ear Granny,*

The weather here is turning mighty cold. All that was said about Global Warming in the papers just can't be true. One more reason to trust the Farmer's Almanac.

I need your advice on two matters. First of all, you spin wool from your sheep. Are sheep easy to care for? Malachi is trying to find ways to make more money, and I told him about you spinning yarn. The English pay high prices for pure wool yarn, I hear. Is that true? Times are hard and we're looking to expand into any business possible.

Point two. Rachael again. My darling girl is pure sugar one minute, bitter old coffee the next. I am at a loss as to what to say, her moods swing so. Do you think it's grief? They were twins and I fear her grief is somehow different than my own.

Any advice on these matters would be helpful.

Danki for the snicker doodle recipe. They turned out wonderful. Here's a recipe for my favorite cookie.

Mattie

Rocky Road Cookies
2 ¼ c. flour
1 tsp. baking soda
1 c. oleo
¼ c. sugar
2 eggs
1 tsp. vanilla
¾ c. brown sugar
1 pkg. instant chocolate pudding
1 c. chocolate chips
1 c. nuts
Using a wooden spoon, mix all ingredients together. If too sticky, add more flour. Drop spoonfuls onto ungreased cookie sheet. Bake at 350 degrees for 10 minutes.

~*~

A few days later, as Rachael ran to the kindling box outside the schoolhouse, she was taken back. Not only was it filled to the brim, but a letter was in a plastic baggie. How odd. When she opened the envelope and saw a small piece of paper with Samuel's writing on it, her heart leapt for joy for an instant, but soon plummeted down again. She could never be his, but she couldn't resist reading his little words of praise. She opened the folded piece of white paper and read: *You are steadfast, not shaken, even when tragedy strikes.*

She held it to her heart. If only that were true. No, I am selfish, not steadfast and I'm shaken every day.

A green Jeep Wrangler came down the road and Rachael felt the blood drain to her feet. Lloyd Longfellow slowed the car and pulled into the school driveway. When he rolled the window down, she saw his deep blue eyes were sympathetic, kind, yearning. "How are you, Rachael?"

She tried to avoid his gaze, failing utterly. "Alright."

He sighed, letting vapor pour from his mouth. "I see Eli all the time over at Sadie's. I think they're going to get hitched."

"I suppose."

Lloyd smiled. "Too bad Kate can't be there for the wedding. You must miss her a lot…"

"I do…"

"I miss *you*. Why not become my housekeeper again? I could use the company and the house needs some TLC." His eyes were begging.

Rachael's mouth grew dry. "I have school to teach."

"Don't you Amish take turns? I mean, you could find someone else to take your place for a day or two. I pay really well and I'd only need you two days a week."

Rachael felt heat rise in her cheeks. She made little money being a schoolteacher, and everyone knew that, but money wasn't why she taught. "*Nee*, I can't do housekeeping anymore." She shifted and put a hand on her hip. "I've given it up for *goot*."

Lloyd's eyes rounded. "Why?"

"I'm starting a new business with my *mamm*. Spinning yarn." She didn't even want to learn to knit, let alone spin, but it would add income to their family.

"I see. Well, can you recommend anyone?"

More heat rose into her cheeks, making them beet red. "*Nee*." She spun on her heels and started towards the schoolhouse.

"Hey, Rachael, why so snobby?"

Snobby? She clenched her hands and marched towards the schoolhouse, mumbling, "You have some nerve."

~*~

Mattie ran from the mailbox, and the cold wind chased her. When she got inside, she ripped open the letter from Deborah Weaver, anxious for a reply. Rachael's behavior was getting so fickle, it dumfounded Mattie. *Why was she angry that someone asked her to do housework? How odd.* She took a seat in her rocker and read:

Dear Mattie,

The snow has blanketed the earth, but my broccoli, late cabbages, and kale are still peeking through. So, one way to save money, as you know, is to have a garden with late crops. There's nothing like cabbage soup fresh from the garden in November. And can you believe November is upon us?

Concerning sheep, well I'm partial to them. They are dear creatures, but my neighbor doesn't think so. He said sheep are good for one thing: getting sick. If you want to come down and see mine, I can show you the care involved.

Now, Rachael is heavy on my heart. I do those casting off prayers, as my knitting circle friends call them. Casting off is a term used in knitting, and when I was knitting one day, I remembered the scripture, Cast your care upon the Lord for He cares for you. Now, Jeb being a fisherman

21

said that casting a fishing pole is work. You don't cast once and expect a fish. I think it's the same with prayer. Casting our concerns for Rachael will take more than one attempt. I cast my cares about many things throughout the day.

But when I cast Rachael on the Lord, I feel somehow like I need to talk to her face to face. So I extend an invitation to Rachael to come and bake pies with me anytime. Wedding season is busy and I could use help in the kitchen. Truth be told, seems like my girls open up when simply working side by side. Let her know she's welcome and we'll continue to cast her on God, because He cares about her.

Thank you for the Rocky Road Cookie recipe. Here's a thrifty, easy recipe for granola. Nothing fancy and most things can be bought at a dry goods store or things on hand in your pantry.

10 c. oatmeal and dry goods such as left over cereal (smashed in small pieces)
2 c. wheat germ or other dry ingredient on hand such as corn meal, sesame seeds, wheat flour
2. c. coconut
2 c. brown sugar (light or dark)
2 c. nuts or seeds such as sunflower seeds, almonds, walnuts (whatever is on hand)
½ c. oil
½ c. honey
1 Tbs. vanilla
1 tsp. salt

Mix above ingredients together, put on cookie trays, and toast at 300 degrees until golden brown. Be careful to flip mixture to prevent burning. (20-30 minutes)
Raisins, dates, and other dried fruits can be added after granola is done baking.
I call this "Everything But the Kitchen Sink Granola", since I throw in everything but!

Granny Weaver

Mattie held the letter to her heart. She would have Rachael spend a day with Granny after Eli's wedding in two weeks. If she protested, Mattie could say that she needed to help an elderly woman in need. Granny did need help baking after all.

~*~

After the three hour church service, Samuel was pleased that Rachael came to him first with her tray of sandwiches. Did she prefer him above the other men who vied for her attention? When she handed him a sandwich, he grabbed her wrist. "Can I ask you something?"

Rachael's pale blue eyes seemed spooked, but she met his gaze. "What is it, Samuel?"

"Are you going to the singing tonight?"

"*Nee*. I'm too old."

"You're only twenty and I'm older than you. How about we both go and take a ride afterwards."

"It's so cold."

Samuel was elated that she hadn't flat out said no. Was his compliment box working? Was her confidence and ability to trust increasing by simple words? If so, words were awfully powerful and he needed to choose them wisely to win her. "We got some snow out there and I have a sleigh. We could take a ride this afternoon."

Her eyes brightened. "*Ach*, I do love a sleigh ride. But it's freezing."

"I can put a sack of hot potatoes under the seat and my buggy robe is thick. We'll be warm as toast."

"I don't know."

"How about just a short ride for half an hour?"

Her features softened and a smile broke across her face. "But it's so much work hitching up a sleigh and all for only half an hour."

"Not a problem at all."

"Okay. When will you pick me up?"

"Well, it gets dark early now. How about three?"

"That's *goot*," she said, her eyes soft as cotton, and turned to offer sandwiches to other men, until she needed to return to the kitchen to replenish her tray.

Samuel bit into his sandwich, and looked across the benches that made a make-shift table. Zeke Byler glared at him, mocking him. "You think Rachael and you could make a match?"

"*Ya*, I do. Why?"

He scratched his freckled chin. "Well, let me warn you from experience. You may catch her for a month or so, but she'll slip away." He leaned forward and whispered, "Take my advice. Don't waste your time on Rachael. Why not go after one of the Troyer girls? All mighty pretty."

Samuel groaned. Zeke was right. Rachael was like a bear in hibernation only coming out from time to time. But maybe today he could convince her to stop hiding from him for good.

~*~

Mattie squeezed Rachael's mitten-covered hands. "Oh, Rachael, I'm ever so pleased to see you going out with Samuel. Have a *goot* time."

Rachael hugged her *mamm*. "Danki, but it's only for half-an-hour. I read that getting outside, even when it's cold, for half-an-hour each day is *goot* for the nerves. So, that's what I'm doing."

Her *mamm's* countenance fell. "Samuel has gone to all the trouble of hitching up the sleigh. No one uses the sleigh until January or February. *Ach, Dochder,* can't you see? Samuel loves you."

If he knew the real me, he would run for the hills, Rachael thought, cringing. "I want to teach. Married women don't teach."

Mattie held her at arms-length, gripping her shoulders firmly. "You are a baptized member of the Amish church. Amish women your age get married. It's God's plan for us to wed and raise a family. Why do you resist the notion?"

Rachael blinked rapidly. Her *mamm* had never been so frank with her concerning marriage. What could she say? The truth? No, it would break her heart. "*Mamm,* I need more time to heal."

Mattie's set her jaw firm. "I miss Kate too. Every day I still see her skipping into the kitchen when she was a little girl, asking to make pies. But we move forward."

"Well, I'm trying, but feel like a wagon wheel that keeps spinning in the mud."

"Cast all your cares on God, Rachael. He cares for you and will lift you out of the... fishing hole."

Rachael cocked her head back. "What?"

"*Ach*, I said it all wrong. Something Granny said about fishing and casting. We need to cast our cares on the Lord because He cares about us. She learned from Jeb, her husband, that when he casts his pole into his fishing hole, he needs to do it over and over. It's hard work." She grasped Rachael's hands. "Keep casting all your sorrow on God. He cares about you and promises to lift our burdens."

Rachael shook her head and then stared at the rubber doormat that she was standing on. *Welcome.* No, God did not welcome her, not after what she'd done.

Karen Anna Vogel

CHAPTER 3

A Rocky Road

Samuel stared straight ahead, as Rachael resisted him putting his arm around her. Why did he even bother with such a temperamental girl? Maybe he *should* consider one of the Troyer sisters.

"I'm sorry, Samuel. I've been rude."

He wanted to agree and say his patience was like thin ice, ready to break. "We were so close growing up. Don't you remember?"

"I do."

Silence. Tree branches heavy laden with snow broke in the woods on either side of the quiet dirt road.

"You deserve someone better."

Samuel nudged her playfully, trying to lighten the mood. "Come on you're as pretty as they come."

"*Nee*, I am not." She looked down and grinned, shyly. "My nose has an arch in it."

Pleased that Rachael was like a clam opening up, he laughed. "Your nose? Are you serious? Your nose is, well, like anyone else's."

She pointed to the bridge of her nose. "It arches right there."

Samuel stared but saw no arch. "*Yinz* women are too hard on yourselves. I never even noticed your nose, and I'd be mighty shallow if I didn't love a girl because her nose wasn't perfect." He reached for her hand under the buggy robe and to his delight she clenched it.

"Samuel, you're too *goot* for me. That's the plain and simple truth."

"Your confidence is too low. Isn't my compliment box working at all?"

"It is."

"Really?"

"Yes. I love it."

Samuel slowed the horse down to a walking pace. He put his arm around her and she leaned her head on his shoulder. Warmth filled his heart and he tilted her chin up, kissing her on her nose. "I love you, Rachael. I always have. Why you've always turned me down in the past is a mystery. Not that I'm the best looking man or anything," he said, wryly. "Well, when you courted freckle- faced Zeke, that did make me wonder, though."

Rachael laughed. "I didn't mean to make you feel bad. You're more handsome than Zeke, but like I said, you deserve someone better."

Samuel shook his head. "I know Kate's death has thrown you off kilter, but I want to help you. Help carry that burden you have on your back, by being your husband."

Tears pooled in Rachael's eyes. "It's my heart, Samuel. It's numb and cold."

"The death of a sister would do that. I understand and will be patient."

A sob escaped Rachael. "I'm not good enough for you."

"I don't want anyone else." He raised her chin again and kissed her quivering lips tenderly. When she didn't resist, he kissed her again, with the passion he had pent up in him for too long, and she recoiled. "I'm sorry, I was too forward."

Fear glazed over her eyes. "Take me home."

Samuel put a hand to her cheek. "I'm so sorry, but I love you, Rachael."

Her eyes begged with him to understand, but she quickly darted her gaze downward. "Samuel, please take me home."

Samuel withdrew his hand away as if bit by a snake. "*Ach*, Rachael, there is a limit to a man's patience." He urged his horse along, picking up speed and soon racing.

Rachael held on, as snow flied up in her face. "Samuel, slow down."

But he only sped up.

~*~

Dear Deborah,

Rachael is worse than ever. She keeps breaking down crying. Is she upset that she's not married as Eli's wedding approaches? I'd like to hire a driver and visit next Wednesday. Can you write as soon as possible to let me know if that's a good day? Weddings being on Tuesdays and Thursdays, I thought it would be a free day for you.

Mattie

~*~

Samuel twiddled his thumbs, waiting for his *daed's* sage advice. He took in the aroma of freshly baked bread, chicken, and corn that his *mamm* was preparing in the kitchen, and his stomach rumbled.

Leaning his head back on his Amish rocker, Matthew Miller bit his lower lip. "Well, *danki* for confessing to me. Driving at such a speed could have flipped the sleigh at the 'black ice' corner, you know."

The scene of the fatal accident that took the life of little Emma Sue Coblentz, at the tender age of seven, on the sharp turn covered with ice, played out in Samuel's mind. Anger was a wrong, and only overtook him on rare occasions if provoked, and Rachael encouraging one minute to pursue her, and then reject him was infuriating.

"Well," his *daed* said, "no one was hurt, and we move forward." He took out his pipe, lit it, and let out a veil of smoke. "Something deeper is wrong with Rachael, I figure. Her behavior sounds more like guilt than grief."

His *daed* offered him a puff on his pipe, but Samuel declined. "How so, *Daed*?"

"Well, grief's an odd thing, bringing out lots of emotion." He scratched his bearded chin. "The day Kate died, there was an ice storm and it was such a horrible thing. Some folks feel that bad things happen because of something wrong they've done. That God is punishing them somehow. Rachael may blame herself for her sister's death. I'm not saying that's what happened, but many things could be causing guilt. Maybe the twins argued before Kate left."

Samuel swallowed hard. "But surely Rachael knew Kate loved her."

"Little Emma Sue's parents, the whole family, suffered from guilt after the Lord took the little angel. Depression, too."

"I remember. But, I've done everything I know to do for Rachael." Samuel glared hopelessly out the window.

"Well, you never thought of guilt. Now you can steer your course in a different direction. Help her get over her guilt and see if it works."

Samuel rubbed the knot in his neck. "Women are work."

"*Ya*, they are, and they feel the same about us."

~*~

The snow melted as an Indian summer spread across Troutville. Rachael sat next to her *mamm* as the wedding vows were exchanged in Sadie's parent's large farmhouse. Her brother, Eli, looked at his bride with tender, loving eyes, and Rachael thought of Samuel. He looked at her like that, too. His attempts over the past week to help relieve her of guilt seemed to make a dent in the way she viewed her past sin. It was in the past, and she needed to move forward. God was loving and forgiving, like all those scriptures Samuel showed her in his well-worn Bible. She needed to open hers from time to time.

After the vows came the wedding feast and Rachael was eager to help, finding new vitality in work. When asked if she could go next door to the *dawdyhaus* and bring down the wedding cake, she hesitated at first, wondering if she'd trip and ruin the little two-tiered cake, but she pushed such nonsense aside and headed out the back door, toward to *dawdyhaus*.

"Rachael, I was hoping to see you alone."

Rachael froze and then slowly turned to face Lloyd Longfellow. "I can't talk to you."

He ran to her and took her by the wrist. "I miss you."

"Leave me alone," she blurted.

"Don't run from me." He rubbed her arm with his other hand. "I noticed you looked lonely when Eli said his vows. Come visit me…"

Heat rose into her cheeks. "I need to go. And what we did was wrong. "

"Rachael, there's nothing wrong with showing love, like I told you."

"Some love is forbidden."

"But isn't love from God? Remember you told me that."

"I was deceived. It was not love."

"It was love, Rach."

"I need to get the cake. Let me go."

Lloyd released her arm but walked beside her towards the *dawdyhaus*. "Can we talk in private?"

"*Nee.*"

"Don't you miss me?"

"Rachael," Samuel yelled from the farmhouse. "Are you alright?"

Samuel. The one she really loved was always there. But she dare not ask for help because he might guess her secret the way Lloyd looked at her. That same look when Lloyd pursued her, when she helped him move in, along with Kate. He told her she was the prettier one... things she wanted to hear. She'd given in to the passion he showed, tricking herself into thinking it was alright. *How could she be so blind?*

Samuel drew near as she said nothing, feeling like she was in a horrible dream. "Rachael, you look sick."

"I need something to drink. It's so hot."

Samuel studied Lloyd's face. "Did you upset her?"

"No, just friendly chatter. Not real comfortable at an Amish wedding but I've known Sadie's folks since I moved in a year or so ago."

Samuel chewed on his lower lip. "How do you know Rachael?"

"Kate and I did housekeeping for him, helping him settle and all," Rachael said, hoping to end this conversation. "Samuel, can you help me carry the cake down? I'm afraid I'll drop it."

Samuel kept his eyes on Lloyd, staring hard. "Alright."

CHAPTER 4

A Visit

A week later, Rachael found herself relieved to finally be in Granny Weaver's kitchen. The scent of baking pies filled the air and Granny was as sweet as the shoofly pie baking in the oven. Her *mamm* had gone out to the barn to learn all there was to learn about sheep from Jeb, but Rachael couldn't help but think this was all planned. Her *mamm* had so many hopes of Granny fixing her.

"The girls at Forget-Me-Not Manor love pies," Granny said with a sense of satisfaction. "We'll take a break for tea. Do you like spearmint?"

"*Ya*, I do. *Danki.*"

"I grow it, you know. Hang it up to dry and then break it up and put it in this here glass canister." She took a large jar out of her cupboard. "And with Jeb having a bee hive, well, this drink is free."

"*Mamm* tells me you're so frugal and thinks you should give classes."

Granny spun around and chuckled. "Your *mamm* knows how to pinch pennies better than she thinks. She just has more mouths to feed. But now that Eli's married and, well, your dear sister gone…"

"It's only me in the house and I want to contribute more than a meager teachers' pay."

Granny cranked the hand pump and water filled her tea kettle. "You have no plans to marry?"

Rachael felt her chin start to quiver so she covered it with her hand. "*Nee*, I feel like I'm supposed to teach. *Kinner* need guidance today."

Granny put the teapot on the stove and sat across from Rachael at her long oak table. "Parents guide *kinner*, you know that. What's the real reason you don't want to wed? Haven't found the right man?"

Rachael looked into Granny's pale blue eyes. They were the same color as Kate's and they seemed to pull at her heart. "A man has proposed but I said no."

"*Ach*, I did that several times. My dear *daed* sent me here to Smicksburg to find a husband and get me away from someone who was tripping me."

"Tripping you?"

"*Ya*, an old beau who turned *English*. He wanted me to follow him into the fancy world, and but by the grace of God, I didn't."

By the grace of God? What kind of talk was that? "Granny, so you're saying you were tempted but didn't give in?"

Granny pointed a finger up. "God helped me or I would have left. I thought I was in love and like they say, love is blind."

"Love is blind? Who says that?"

Granny pursed her lips and then a grin broke out. "I'm sorry. I have many *English* friends and I pick up their sayings. 'Love is blind' means that you can't see things clearly when in love, or in lust, as I was."

Rachael gasped. "Lust?"

"*Ya*, lust. I'm human."

"Did you...fall?"

"What do you mean by fall?"

Rachael felt like putting her head outside into the cold November snow, blushing profusely. "You know what I mean."

"Ach. I did in my heart, which is just as bad as if we'd been intimate." Granny reached for her hand. "Rachael, you have fallen?"

Rachael felt her heart leap into her throat. "What makes you think such a thing?"

"I'm a woman," Granny said. "I can sense things."

"Does my *mamm* suspect this, too? Is that why she has me here?"

Granny stroked her hand. "*Nee*, your *mamm* is too close to you to see such a thing, but I just met you so I don't get mixed signals."

"What do you mean?"

"Ach, my boys could pull the wool over my eyes. I loved them all so and thought the best, like a *mamm* does. When someone pointed out some odd behavior one of my *kinner* had, I'd brush it aside like lint. Jeb stepped in and could seem to see things more clearly. *Ya*, a *mamm's* heart can love too much, making us see our *kinner* in a different light."

Rachael swallowed hard. "You think I'm not pure then?"

"I suspect you're not. Your eyes tell me you hold a lot of guilt." Granny got up as the whistle blew and poured hot water into two teacups, adding spearmint tea to both, a dab of honey and then placed them on the table. "You can tell me, Rachael. We all have feet of clay, able to fall. I don't judge."

Feet of clay that can fall... "And when we fall, we are forgiven?"

"*Ya*, but we need to confess any wrongdoing and let others help us get back on our feet. You see, when you put a seed in the ground, it can't grow unless there's water. That seed only sees darkness all around it. But when water comes, it gets plumped up and begins to feel life again. You follow my meaning?"

"Not really. Some of it."

"When you hide yourself and your sin, you die inside, like that seed. Seeds are dead, you know. But water brings them back to life. The love of God and others bring us back to life."

"But others will never understand..."

"They might." Granny grabbed for her hand again. "We carry each other's burdens. Let me help you. Confession is *goot* for the soul."

A sob escaped Rachael and she felt for the first time in a year she could tell someone what she'd done. Granny was so gentle and she felt so safe. "I did sin, and that sin killed my sister."

"Start from the beginning and tell me what happened."

"Well, Kate and I were housekeepers for a new bachelor in town who inherited a large house. Our family needed more money to put towards our tax bill. This *Englisher* paid us so much, being very wealthy now. One day Kate couldn't make it and I went alone. Lloyd and I talked a lot. The next day, Kate couldn't come again, and he made advances on me."

"How old were you?" Granny asked, hand on her heart.

"I was almost nineteen."

"Did he force himself on you?"

Filth filled Rachael's heart as she tried to remember how it all started. "*Nee*, I gave in. He told me how lonely he was in the big old house and wanted to meet the right girl. Told me I was pretty." Tears filled her eyes. "He led me to his bedroom and I followed."

"Did you put up a fuss?" Granny asked evenly.

"*Nee*, that's the worst part. I don't know what overcame me, but I found pleasure in it." She covered her face with her hands, shame filling her.

"And how long did this go on?"

"Only once. He asked me to come back and I said no, never again. Kate seemed to see through me and up and asked me what was wrong, and I admitted everything. And that's what killed her."

"How so?" Granny prodded.

"She rode to the quilt shop the next morning and got in an accident. She was distracted because of my confession."

"Your *mamm* said there was an ice storm." Granny came around the table and sat next to her, rubbing her back. "Now, the Lord has a time to take us all. Not one sparrow can fall without him knowing about it, and he cares for us more than birds. It was Kate's time."

"She was too *goot* to die."

"Maybe she was so *goot* she was ready to meet the Lord."

Rachael slowly met Granny's loving gaze. "Do you think God caused the accident then?"

"Well, I wouldn't go that far. He's a loving parent and no parent wants to see harm come to their *kinner*. But they do, however, since we live in a fallen world, not the Garden of Eden anymore."

Rachael's brows creased. "You really think there was a real garden where everything was perfect?"

"I believe every word in my Bible and that's what it says. Do you think God could create a world with so much evil?"

Rachael shook her head, "*Nee*, I suppose not."

Granny rubbed her back. "Now, let's get back to when you started to stray."

"Stray?"

"*Ya*, you have strayed from the straight and narrow path God had you on."

"Well, like I said, I let Lloyd lead me into sin."

"Let's step back first. Lloyd is a man who tempted you. He lured you in like a fish." Granny motioned towards the window. "You can see we have a fishing pond in our backyard for Jeb, so I know all about fishing and lures. This man used the lure of sympathy on a sympathetic Amish girl first, I'm thinking."

"Sympathy?"

"If he asked you the first day you went to clean to follow him to his room, would you have gone?"

"Of course not."

"So he played on your sympathy. Maybe he didn't realize what he was doing. Maybe he was lonely, but he made you feel sorry for him, right?"

"*Ya*, I did…"

"Now, you know premarital sex is forbidden. Did this upset you?"

Rachel took a handkerchief out of her pocket and wiped the sweat forming on her forehead. "*Ya*, it was hard. When I told him I believed in remaining pure until marriage, he laughed. He made me question everything…"

"Go on."

"Well, the more I talked to Lloyd, I began to question everything about Amish ways and…"

"You thought God was withholding something from you. Something you deserved."

Rachael couldn't believe how Granny could read her thoughts. "Exactly."

"It's the same story told a million different ways. God has a plan for us, like Adam and Eve in the garden. Satan comes in and says, 'Go ahead and take that fruit that God is withholding from you.

He's not as good as you think He is. He's trying to keep real happiness and joy from you.'" Granny snarled. "He's a sly one. He first tries to get you to think that God isn't good."

Rachael thought back to the well-known Bible story. God placed Adam and Eve in the garden but they needed free will so he told them not to eat from one tree, but they did anyhow. But Rachael did more than eat an apple, she lost her virginity. "Granny, I see what you mean, but my sin has made it impossible for me to marry."

"Why?"

"Who would want a wife like me?" Rachael exclaimed.

"We all stumble and fall, no sin is bigger than the other. God looks at your heart."

Rachael stared into her spearmint tea. "What should I do?"

"Well, you need to make a confession."

"In front of the whole church?"

"It's our way. There's a price to pay for sin."

Rachael had prayed that God would lead her out of guilt, but the way out seemed worse than anything. How could she do a kneeling confession? No, she could not. But just having someone else know her secret did seem to lighten her load…

~*~

Mattie stroked the top of the ram's head. "He doesn't bite, ya?"

"Only if you taste *goot*," Jeb chuckled. "*Nee*, they are gentle creatures, but not too smart."

"How so?"

"They need guidance and I can see why Psalm twenty-three says that the Lord is our shepherd, He leads us beside still waters. Sheep need a leader who is *goot*, or else they'll just follow the most dominate sheep. I've seen sheep topple down a hill because one sheep led them down a steeper path to the barn."

"Did they get hurt?" Mattie asked.

"*Nee*, it was comical." He pointed to the hill towards the back of his land. "It's not a steep cliff, just a slope. But it always reminds me that we need a shepherd."

Mattie leaned against the stall. "I'm hoping Granny can lead my Rachael back to peace. Somehow I feel she blames herself for her sister's death."

Jeb looped his thumbs through his suspenders. "Well, I can relate. When Deborah had the stillborn girl, I blamed myself. If only I'd had her give birth in a hospital. If only I'd seen some signs of distress. I was much younger, but I started to wonder, if only I was a better man. Now I know all the 'if only's' make us sink into depression. Faith made me see that God took our little one straight to heaven. Sometimes we need to read our Bibles to see clearly."

If only... Mattie had her list of 'if only's' scribbled in her mind. *If only* she'd paid attention to the weather like her husband warned, *if only* they weren't so greedy for money, Kate wouldn't have sold the quilt that day. "Jeb, I can see why Samuel writes to you. You're a wise man."

"Wise old man, Deborah would say." He smirked. "Now why would you come out and say something like that? You'll make me proud."

Mattie's mood darkened. "I've blamed myself for Kate's death. My husband warned about an ice storm coming in, but Kate insisted and I, needing money from the quilt sale for groceries, agreed with Kate. I encouraged her and look what happened."

Jeb put a hand up. "Guilt and condemnation aren't from God. They can make you go mad. Like I said, the truth is found in God's Word and the truth is that He has the power over life and death, not us. Your Kate is skipping around heaven I'd say, according to what the Bible says."

Mattie's eyes widened. "Did you say skipping?"

Well, I have three *grandkinner* who skip a lot so I imagine Kate being carefree and skipping like the girls."

"*Ach*, Jeb. You didn't know Kate skipped all the time, even at eighteen?"

"*Nee*, I did not."

"Then it's a sign from God that you said that. Kate is skipping in heaven."

Jeb's eyes mellowed into blue pools. "If it comforts you, I'm glad. But what God has to say about heaven, especially in the last three chapters of the Bible, are what is real and will comfort the most. You read it and see. The end of a book is always the best."

"*Ya*, I suppose." Mattie smiled and watched a barn swallow swoop through the barn and land in a rafter. "Have you heard from Samuel lately?"

"He's a fine fellow, but troubled. He loves Rachael, you know, but a man's patience can run thin. I'm praying that Rachael won't let him get away."

51

"That's what I keep saying, but she says she wants to be single and teach, but then when I see her with Samuel, I see the love in her eyes."

"I've learned that a *mamm's* intuition has power. My Deborah seems to have a sixth sense about couples getting together and maybe you can sense something, too. Have you told Samuel you believe Rachael loves him?"

"Heaven's no. It's not my place."

~*~

Relieved that Jeb offered to show Rachael sheep after dinner, Mattie was anxious to talk to Granny alone. As they took their coffee into the living room, and Jeb and Rachael went outside, Mattie took a sideways glance again at Granny. Yes, she had worry etched on her face, as did Rachael. What was wrong? "Did you get to the root of Rachael's problem? She's carrying guilt?"

The room having several rocking chairs and benches in a circle, Granny sat across from Mattie. "*Ya*, lots of guilt."

"Over her sister's death. What did you tell her?"

Granny stared into her mug. "Mattie, sometimes our *kinner* surprise us. They do things we never thought possible."

Mattie wasn't sure if Granny was trying to brace her for something or wanted to change the subject. "*Ya*, they do. My oldest boy, Jason, had a *rumspringa* on the wild side."

"What did he do?" Granny asked.

"Well, he and some other buddies hitched a ride to a bar. He drank and you know what that leads to."

"*Nee*, I do not. Drunk driving?"

"Immorality, like the Bible says. Strong drink makes you do things you're later ashamed of."

Granny looked out the window, avoiding eye contact. "So did you forgive Jason?"

"Of course. He wasn't a baptized member of the church and only sixteen. And I'm Amish, so we forgive."

"*Ya*, we do. We know that we are made of dust and are all able to fall." Granny met Mattie's gaze at last. "Your *dochder* will be needing the same mercy you showed Jason."

Mattie slowly set her mug on its saucer. "What are you saying?"

"Rachael's a sweet girl who someone lured in like a fish. Now brace yourself because your *dochder* needs help." Granny let out a sigh. "Do you know of a man named Lloyd, who Kate and Rachael kept a house for?"

Mattie felt her stomach flip. "You mean someone took advantage of Rachael?"

"I've never had a *dochder* so I can't relate to your pain. Rachael consented to immorality with a man named Lloyd."

Mattie knew Granny was aging but was she going completely daft? "I don't believe that," she blurted.

"He seduced her. She was alone with him and Rachael gave in to sexual sin."

Mattie shot up a hand. "Stop. This can't be true."

"The truth sets you free to help your *dochder*," Granny said in even tones. "Now, she's not only feeling the guilt of that, but the guilt of her sister's death. She told Kate after it happened and Kate went out the next day needing some time to reflect, I suppose." Granny's eyes misted. "That's when the accident happened."

Mattie wanted to get up and scream and accuse Granny of losing her mind, but her face registered grief and concern, and great love for Rachael. "She told you this?"

"*Ya*, she did, and no one else and all that pent up guilt is destroying her."

"How could she?" Mattie shouted, her chin shaking. "I didn't raise her to be a loose woman. A Delilah sleeping at Samson's feet." She shot up and paced the room. "Kate would never do such a thing." Stamping a foot, she let out more rage. "I've told Rachael I blamed myself for Kate's death, not abiding by my husband's wishes, needing money from the quilt we made. How could Rachael be so cruel?"

Granny ran over to Mattie and took her hand. "Sin starts as a little thing but can grow. Rachael's shame made her bury herself. She looked inward too much, getting depressed, and most likely didn't even hear you blame yourself."

Mattie shook her head. "I don't know my *dochder*."

"You don't know the grip sin and guilt can have on a life. Now, you sit down and I'll get some pie. This has been an awful shock, but we need to talk more about how we can restore Rachael. She's baptized and will need to confess this sin to your bishop and elders…"

CHAPTER 5

A Confession

*D*ecember winds beat against Rachael's bedroom window, but sunlight poured in as well, lifting her spirits. Last week, after much talk between her *mamm* and *daed*, they decided to extend forgiveness. Although they looked at her with disappointment, Rachael felt guilt ease its grip on her heart. *Mold grows in dark places*, Granny had said, *and so did guilt. Bringing it out in the open was the first step in killing it.*

She shook her head as she thought of how Samuel would react to her confession. Today was enough to think about, though, confessing her sin to the bishop and elders. Take it step by step, Granny had said. *Live each hour for God and the years will take care of themselves*, Jeb had advised. But the icy clutch of fear yanked her emotions. What if she had to confess in front of the whole *Gmay*?

Rachael ran over to her desk, reading again the letter that Granny had written to her so she could prepare for her confession.

My Dear Sweet Rachael,

The girls at Forget-Me-Not Manor enjoyed our pies and they wanted me to send along their thanks. I hope you can come back down and help me again.

Now, concerning your confession before the bishop and elders, I have this advice. Hold your head up high. King David was a man after God's own heart and fell into fornication. Now, you have your whole life ahead of you so don't let one sin on one day ruin all that is before you. A husband and kinner are the real blessings in life, and I pray your Samuel will understand.

I want you to memorize these verses.

There is therefore now no condemnation to them which are in Christ Jesus, who walk not after the flesh, but after the Spirit. Romans 8:1

Broken down, this here verse says you're blameless. Think about that. You stumble and fall but when your heart is following the Holy Spirit, God forgives. He loves you and knows you have feet of clay, like I said.

Even before He made the world, God loved us and chose us in Christ to be holy and without fault in His eyes. Ephesians 1:4

Honey, God knew you in your mother's womb and loves you. When we confess sin, He sees us without fault. How I love that. It's an awfully powerful thing.

Come now, and let us reason together, saith the LORD: though your sins be as scarlet, they shall be as white as snow; though they be red like crimson, they shall be as wool. Isaiah 1:18

Now Rachael, this is one of my favorite verses in the Bible. Can you guess why? Of course you can, it has wool in it. I know the cleansing process wool goes through before it touches my spinning wheel, so being clean is a process. We need washing daily. But scarlet is a mighty hard stain to get out of anything. Ever spill berry juice on a tablecloth when canning? I have. It's a permanent stain, but God does the impossible and gets stains out of our souls. And remember, He does it because He loves us.

Now, when you face the bishop and elders, you be honest and confess, holding back nothing. Remember to tell them how you were lured and he played on your sympathy. They will let you know if they believe you need to confess to the whole Gmay, but I'm thinking it won't be necessary. Let's hope it stays with those God has put over you to shepherd you.

Ever in my prayers,

Granny Weaver

Rachael held the letter to her heart and prayed for strength as she faced the bishop and elders gathered downstairs. Would they be as understanding as Granny?

~*~

Rachael sat in the living room while the bishop and two elders perched on their chairs, gazing at her like startled birds. Bishop John yanking at his long gray beard leaned over, staring at the floor, grunting and shifting his lean weight. The pendulum clock's usual dainty tick-tock was now an annoyance, accentuating the silence.

"Well Rachael," Bishop John said gravely, "seems like your compassion got distorted. You felt sorry for a lonely man, but comforted him in a sinful way."

Rachael attempted to talk but found the strength hard to muster. She met Elder Alan's misty eyes.

"Bishop, this family has carried a hefty load, losing Kate, and I believe restoration is needed." He opened his black leather Bible, flipped through pages, and cleared his throat:

"Isaiah talks about Judah being unfaithful to God, but it ended with hope.

"Come now, let us settle the matter," says the Lord.

"Though your sins are like scarlet, they shall be as white as snow;

"though they are red as crimson, they shall be like wool.

"If you are willing and obedient, you will eat the good things of the land;

"but if you resist and rebel, you will be devoured by the sword."

Elder Alan kept his eyes on his Bible. 'Now, it ends with a choice. Reason together with God, ask forgiveness and turn from sin, or resist God and rebel. I believe Rachael could have taken this secret into her grave, bearing shame in her heart. But she has chosen to face us and ask for forgiveness. I say we extend it."

Rachael's heart raced as the good elder said these words, but Elder Adam had been rather cool and quiet.

"Are we in agreement then?" the Bishop asked, looking over at Adam. "I believe enough has befallen this household to cause pain. God's love covers a multitude of sin, and we must walk in His steps."

Elder Adam pursed his lips and fidgeted with the edge of his shirt sleeve. "I have a confession to make. My *dochder*, Emma, went over when Lloyd first moved in, to keep house and such. She said Lloyd was a charmer, and felt uneasy, so never went back. Soon after, I saw Rachael and Kate going over regular-like, but I never said anything. I should have protected these little lambs. *Ach,* Rachael, I'm so sorry."

Rachael gripped the edge of her chair. "I should have told my parents, like your *dochder* did. I allowed him to lure me in."

"Why, Rachael? Think back as to why," Bishop John instructed. "Sin starts as a seed and grows."

It baffled Rachael why she didn't resist Lloyd. "I don't really know. I remember thinking no one could be happy with a girl like me."

"Why not?" Elder Alan asked.

"I'm not pretty enough."

The bishop leaned forward. "And what makes you think that?"

"Kate was the beauty, not me."

Elder Alan gasped. "Is that why you broke things off with Zeke? Not feeling *goot* enough?"

Kate shook her head. "I was tired of people asking when I'd court someone, so I courted Zeke for a while. It was dishonest. I never cared for him."

The constant beat of the pendulum clock helped Rachael take even breaths.

"Rachael, is your confession over?" Bishop John asked.

Rachael nodded, heat rising from her neck then onto her cheeks. How humiliating this had been.

The men nodded in agreement with each other.

"We forgive you, sister. Now go and sin no more." Bishop John stood up and took Rachael's hand. "And if you should ever feel tempted to sin again, you know you must flee. Flee from evil, the Bible says."

Rachael felt her sweaty palm being tightened by the good Bishop. "I will."

Elder Adam asked for forgiveness again for not warning her about Lloyd and Elder Alan embraced her like a *daed*, and then the three men made their way out of the side door.

Rachael felt spent, but her heart was starting to experience something she hadn't felt in over a year: Joy.

~*~

Samuel leaned into the wind as he made his way to the mailbox. After retrieving some taxidermy catalogs, he saw that Jeb Weaver had sent another letter. Samuel hurried back inside, left the mail on the table for his *mamm* to see, and then sat next to the warmth of the woodstove. Opening Jeb's letter, he read:

Samuel,

I met some folks up your way. Mattie and Rachael Yoder. Mighty fine women. I suppose they want to buy some sheep come spring to make yarn for extra money. Well, it's my wife's addiction I must live with. Some things in marriage you just turn the cheek, although when Deborah makes me a fine wool hat and scarf, I give her a peck on her cheek. That's a joke if you know what I mean.

I can see why you've taken a liking to Rachael. She's a pretty girl with a good heart. Now, not perfect, mind you. It takes a mighty strong person to face themselves and admit to a wrong. My advice to you is to be a strong person and slow down... confession is good for the soul.

Your friend,

Jeb Weaver

Samuel pulled off his black brimmed hat and then raked his fingers through his light brown hair. *Confess?* What did he have to confess? Jeb's letter made no sense. Slow down? Samuel had revealed how much he was making per deer head. Was he working too much? But he needed to make a living.

His *daed* joined him as they waited for the noon meal to be prepared. "What's wrong? Bad news?"

Samuel leaned his head back on his rocker and stared aimlessly. "Jeb Weaver's not making sense. He's encouraging me to confess for something I don't know about."

"Jeb's a wise man. What do *yinz* write about?"

"Well, to be honest, women. I mean, he talks about his wife and I talk about..."

"Rachael?"

"*Ya*, and about the maple syrup and taxidermy. Is it wrong to be so ambitious?"

Matthew Miller yanked at his salt and pepper beard. "Can be. We Millers are known to be hard workers and your uncle did have to quit his job at the mill because he made too much."

Samuel shook his head but said nothing. His uncle had eight *kinner* at the time and needed money. From writing to his pen pal in Lancaster, Samuel knew that he was nearly a millionaire, although he gave most of it to the community. When he saw how much Rachael's family struggled, he thought maybe having a few millionaire Amish in Troutville would benefit them.

Raising sheep for extra money? Rachael stayed home to quilt enough as it was. Samuel's heart did a flip. Did the family need money so badly that they depended on Rachael's salary? If she married, they'd lose the income she provided from her teaching position. Samuel felt like he just discovered the root of Rachael's sour disposition over the past year. *She had to teach and didn't like it.*

"What exactly did Jeb's letter say concerning sin?" Matthew prodded.

Looking over the letter again, Samuel read, "My advice to you is to be a strong person. And slow down… confession is good for the soul."

Matthew shook his head. "Did you mention how fast you drove the sleigh?"

"*Nee*, I did not." Taking a deep breath, he sighed. "But Rachael's *mamm* writes to Jeb's wife. Mattie must have mentioned it." Samuel leaned his head against the rocker again, looking up. Racing a horse wasn't a sin. During *rumspringa,* he and his buddies raced on dirt roads for miles.

CHAPTER 6

A Wrong Turn

After Sunday service a few days later, Samuel's heart beat against his ribs when Rachael served him first.

"Want some coffee to warm you up?" she quipped.

"*Ya. Danki.*" Rachael's eyes seemed more hopeful, so Samuel knew the notes he left over at her place yesterday, the compliments to put in her box, must have lifted her spirits. "What are you doing today?"

Rachael pursed her lips. "There's lots of snow outside. Would be fun to go sledding on Goosedown Hill."

Zeke, who sat across from Samuel, cleared his throat. "Samuel, I've asked the Troyer girls to go sledding."

Samuel cocked his head in disbelief, and then he tried not to glare at him. Zeke didn't want him to waste his time on Rachael, but he had no interest in any other girl. Peering up at Rachael, it was unmistakable. Pain was etched into her light blue eyes, making them ice. "Rachael, would you like to go sledding with us?"

Rachael's chin started to quiver. "*Nee*. Don't want to intrude."

Zeke shoved Samuel's foot under the table. "*Danki*, Rachael. My sled's only cozy for four."

Samuel gasped as Rachael swiftly nodded and went on to serve the other men coffee.

"She deserves it," Zeke snickered. "Sure got her dander up."

"Zeke, that was deceitful. What's wrong with you?"

"Hey, I got us a double date this afternoon," he said wryly. "Two oldest Troyer girls agreed to go sled-riding with us."

"Us? I wasn't even asked." Samuel clenched his fork and jabbed the pie in front of him.

"Happy Birthday, Buddy. It's your present." Zeke pulled an envelope from his vest pocket. "Use the money to pay for Fern's meal. I'm hooked on Heather."

Samuel was just too dumbfounded to respond, only to say that he was touched his friend remembered his birthday was coming up. But was Zeke that dense? Didn't he believe him that he'd pursue Rachael until he won her?

~*~

Rachael cozied herself in a favorite quilt she and Kate had pieced together. Kate had cut out the pink calico material and Rachael gently traced the outline of the pattern with a finger. Her sister had been her closest friend, and more memories were coming of them playing outside in the sandbox as preschoolers. Of the two of them clinging to each other as they flew down Goosedown Hill, snow flying up at them, nearly being covered at the end of the hill.

She bit her lower lip. Which Troyer sister would Samuel pick? Hurt stung her as she thought of Samuel's betrayal. Just when she was getting brave to say she cared for him, he became as fickle as a school girl. This was another reason why she should consider Granny's offer to have an extended visit over Christmas vacation. The twelve days of Christmas in Smicksburg were maybe something she should consider. She was fearfully and wonderfully made, as Granny had told her. She did deserve a good Amish husband, one filled with mercy and grace, just like Jeb.

Unwrapping herself, Rachael went over to her desk and took out her flower embossed stationery and wrote:

Dear Granny,

I miss you and realize a Christmas visit is what I need. I believe the bishop and elders when they say my past sin is mum with them, but somehow Samuel seems to be drifting away. I have the courage to tell him about my past, but not the opportunity. He's out sledding right now with another girl. So, there's more than one reason I'd like to come to Smicksburg for an extended stay.

The Bible verses you send me are helping more than anything. I can't believe what a sinner King David was, but he was a man after God's own heart. His sins of adultery and murder being cleansed make me walk tall inside. I know I'm forgiven, and the guilt is easing up. But guilt held back sorrow over Kate's death and I'm crying a lot. You're right. Guilt has a way of blinding us, and I'm mourning the death of my sister it seems for the first time.

Rachael stopped the pen that poured out her soul. Christmas in Smicksburg with all its quaint little shops would be a treat. But how could she stay for twelve days? Her parents missed Kate more than ever around the holidays. And Eli wouldn't be home, most likely spending the day with Sadie's side.

Well, she was learning not to fret from dear Granny, so she cast her cares on the Lord, for He cared about her. She left the letter unfinished and went downstairs to discuss her plan with her parents. Christmas was only a week away.

~*~

Samuel never noticed that Fern had eyes like emeralds and such rosy cheeks. As they flew through the snow, her smile came from her heart and this was something he sorely missed in Rachael. As the snow spit up into the toboggan, Fern turned and buried her face in his chest, and he liked it. Little Fern was someone he'd never considered, her being so much younger, but her cheerfulness was something that lifted his spirits.

Samuel thought back to Jeb's letter. *Don't give up if you feel Rachael's the one for you, and extend mercy and grace to the girl. She needs it.* Yes, Rachael was preoccupied with work, trying to make ends meet, and now wanting to add yarn to her list of to-do things. Was she a workaholic, not trusting God to provide, or was the family struggling that badly?

All he knew was that this birthday present of Zeke's had opened his eyes to other available girls, and he wanted a family, and Fern even said she'd come over and help tan leather or even help with all the other dirty work. He did have a squirrel and a bluebird that needed mounted and the clock was ticking to Christmas. His many *English* clients had to have their present the day of Christmas, not extending the holiday over twelve days as the Amish did. Could Fern stomach mounting a dead bird over a mold?

The sled eased into a stop at the bottom of the hill, and Fern looked up at Samuel with a giggle. "You're a snowman, all covered in snow." She brushed the ice crystals off his jacket and then took his hand to steady herself as she got out of the sled.

Zeke glanced over at Samuel, one eyebrow arched. A grin that said, 'See, there's other fish in the sea' almost made Samuel laugh out loud. What a funny freckle-faced guy he was. Did the Lord orchestrate this whole event through this goofy friend of his? Was he to pay more attention to Fern?

"Let's do it again," Fern said, her eyes glistening, snowflakes on her lashes.

Zeke winked at Samuel. "Sure, let's do it again. Let's race up the hill. Heather and I will beat *yinz*." At that he took Heather's hand as they mounted the hill.

"Hey, you left us with the toboggan, Freckles. You have the advantage."

Fern slid her hand into his. "We can still beat them even if we have to haul this thing. My sister's as slow as molasses in January."

Spunk. How Samuel liked that in a girl. He'd never noticed how much he'd missed while pursuing Rachael Yoder.

~*~

Mattie wrapped her arms around Rachael after hearing her request to go to Granny's on Second Christmas. "Won't you miss seeing your own family? Your brothers and sisters will be coming for an extended stay, as usual."

Rachael needed to be more open with her *mamm*. Maybe keeping her faults, hurts and temptations to herself was what caused her to slide into sin. Putting on a smile, a mask, that all was well. "*Mamm*, do you know Samuel is out sledding with the Troyer girls this afternoon?"

Mattie gasped. "*Nee*, I did not. Are you hurt?"

You can do this, Rachael Yoder. Admit a fault. "Yes, I am. Samuel said he'd wait for me no matter what, even proposed marriage."

Clucking her tongue like a morning chicken, Mattie shook her head. "What a pickle. Maybe Granny will have a way of smoothing things over. She was the one who cracked you open like a walnut."

"So you agree, I need to stay with Granny for a while?"

"*Ya*, but I will miss you. Our baking time together and visiting folks, well, it won't be the same. But with no other woman knowing your past... situation... I can see the need. Granny is so full of wisdom. Jeb, too."

Rachael turned to hug her *mamm*, realizing as she shared from her heart, her *mamm* was, too. Why was it so hard to share with people the closest to you?

~*~

Samuel wasn't sure what to make of Fern's behavior. He liked to pursue a girl, not be pursued, and there was something unattractive about her behavior over the past few days. She brushed up against him in his taxidermy shop, looking intently at him as if needing a kiss. Her non-stop chatter about herself also made her seem mighty self-centered. Rachael was so reserved; being a polar opposite, a little extreme in the other way.

"Did you hear Rachael is spending Second Christmas in Smicksburg?" Fern asked with a chuckle. "I think she has a secret beau down there. Word has it she writes often to someone in that settlement."

"Her pen pal lives there. Granny Weaver. I write to her husband, Jeb. Fine folk."

"I know some Weavers. Is the woman's name Deborah?"

"*Ya*, it is."

"Then my suspicions are right. She's a matchmaker."

"What?"

"A matchmaker. Someone who's *goot* at seeing that people need to be together. She has some single nephews down there. Wonder who she has her eye on for Rachael?"

The deer hide Samuel was trying to fit over the mold seemed too small, or was he losing his strength to work by hearing this news? Jeb had encouraged him to extend mercy and grace to Rachael. Was that because Rachael had picked another man? He needed to let her go? She had more of a skip in her step at church. Was she in love with someone from Smicksburg?

Samuel tugged on the fur but it was no use. The mold was too large and he needed to shave it off a bit. Anger filled him and he wanted to throw the whole piece up against the wall. But why the anger if he didn't care about Rachael?

"I'm closing up shop early today. Mighty tired."

Fern put a dainty hand on his back. "Are you alright? You look pale."

"I'm fine. Just tired from all these orders and the *English* being so impatient."

"Does anyone else know how to do taxidermy?"

Samuel shook his head. "*Nee.* Maybe I just need to take a break."

"How about we go have dinner at the Sampler? My treat."

My treat? "*Nee*, I'll pay. I never let a girl pay."

Fern put her hand on his cheek. "So, are we courting?"

Tongue-tied, Samuel said nothing, only gave Fern a slight smile. "Let's get out of here. I've worked too hard." He wanted to add, *alone*. He'd been working in this shop alone for too long. *Lord, send the right mate to me and make it clear that she's your choice, no matter if my heart keeps going back to Rachael.*

CHAPTER 7

A Revelation

*T*he scent of pine filled the one-room schoolhouse, and Rachael noticed Samuel come in to watch her students perform their Christmas Eve program. Why? But when Fern Troyer jumped from her seat, barging through the crowd to make her way to Samuel, Rachael couldn't help but stare. Such a bold girl. Did Samuel like them that way?

"Rachael, Susan Hershberger's crying, saying she's going to vomit," a student said, pulling at Rachael's dress sleeve.

Rachael ran over to Susan. "Honey, are you alright?"

The eight year old girl shook, saying she was too nervous to sing her solo. Rachael hugged her, encouraged her, but in the end, Susan said she couldn't perform.

Rachael knew the closing was special, inviting the audience to participate in a gleeful song of worship. She ran over to another student, who objected, and then another, who also shook in fear at the prospect.

"Will I have to sing it myself?" Rachael mumbled under her breath.

"I'll sing with you, teacher," a small voice said. It was one of her first graders, Lydia Hostetler, pink cheeks aglow.

"Danki, Lydia. Of course, we can sing the song together." She bent down to kiss her plump cheek.

Rachael felt a tap on her shoulder, and turned to see Samuel hovering over her. "Is everything alright?"

Astonished, she managed to tell him how Lydia had saved the program.

Samuel touched her arm. "Can we talk after the program?"

"Won't Fern be upset?" Rachael snapped, and then covered her mouth in aghast. "Ach, I didn't mean to say that. It's just that you're courting and all."

Samuel eye's widened and he shook his head. "She thinks we are, but I'm not too keen on a girl who chases me like a fox in a henhouse."

Rachael puckered her lips as she started to giggle. "That was funny."

"That's the truth. She hen pecks and I'm not even married to her." He winked. "Get it…"

Rachael only laughed harder, his play of words mixed with relief that he wasn't at all interested in Fern made her forget herself. In front of everyone, she took his hand, glowing. "*Ya,* I'd like for you to take me home. We need to talk."

Samuel's face split open with a smile.

Rachael prayed that somehow he'd understand her confession….

~*~

Samuel lit the battery operated lights on his buggy, took Rachael's hand to help her in, all the while Fern stood there gaping.

"I thought you were my ride home, Samuel. My family already left."

Samuel reached for Rachael's hand, grimacing. She looked away, afraid she was going to laugh at Samuel's expression. Snowflakes fell and she opened her mouth to catch one on her tongue. *Though your sins be as scarlet, they shall be as white as snow,* she felt a still small voice inside her say. This Bible verse literally had come alive to her, but would Samuel feel the same way?

Fern sat in the back seat of the buggy, huffing. Samuel asked Rachael if she was warm enough, but not Fern, which made her react with a slug to his arm. "There's more than one girl in this buggy," she griped.

"Are you cold, Fern?" Samuel said in even tones.

"I'm back here by myself and freezing."

"Well, I'm taking you home first, and you don't live far." Samuel carefully guided his horse over to the side of the road to let a car pass. "The program turned out real nice, Rachael. You sing *goot*."

"Danki, but I couldn't have done it without little Lydia by me, not liking all the attention on myself."

Another huff from the backseat. Fern was obviously not enjoying this buggy ride, and Rachael noticed that Samuel had the horse almost galloping to deposit Fern at her house. "Better slow down," she said, "Might be ice under this snow."

Samuel's mood had turned sour with Fern's complaining. When her house came into view, Rachael wondered if it was a good night to make her confession.

Pulling into the Troyer's long driveway, Samuel halted the horse, and told Fern to get out.

"Aren't you going to drive up to my house?"

"Your *daed* hasn't plowed it. We'd get stuck."

"Won't you walk me then? I'm afraid of the dark."

Samuel moaned. "I'm taking Rachael on a ride so we can talk. Understand? I asked Rachael if I could take her home."

Fern put her hands on her hips, looking like a bull ready to charge. "You're courting?"

"I hope so," Samuel said, in a more tender tone. "Fern, you deserve someone who's more like you." He looked up at the full moon. "I think Zeke fits you better than Heather."

She twisted and gave a half smile. "You think so?"

"*Ya*," Samuel said. "And I think he's keen on you."

The sound of horses clip clopping approached and soon some of the Troyer clan appeared, squished into one buggy. "Fern, you can't walk the driveway," her aunt yelled out. "We'll fit you in." Fern tilted her head, as if deep in thought, and then waved goodbye to Samuel and Rachael.

Rachael squeezed Samuel's hand. "I admire you, Samuel. You have a way of smoothing things over. I'm not as *goot* with words."

"Nonsense. Look at what you pulled off tonight at the program. You're a great teacher, but can't hide behind that 'calling' of yours forever."

"I know. But Samuel, I may have to."

"What makes you say that?"

Rachael looked ahead, not able to speak.

Samuel slowed the horse to a walk and then put his arm around her, pulling her near. "I'd be honored to have you as my wife. You know that, and the offer still stands. Marry me, Rachael."

His voice was hopeful and condemnation beat hard against Rachael. She closed her eyes and thought, *There is no condemnation to those in Christ. I'm His child and forgiven.* Taking a deep breath, she said, "Samuel, I sinned a year ago. A few days before Kate died. I got help from Granny Weaver, Jeb's wife, and am going to stay with them over Christmas break to get more help. The bishop, elders, and my family have forgiven me, and I pray you will, too."

Samuel sat up straight. "There's nothing I wouldn't forgive. I must say it's shocking that the bishop and elders had to get involved. Tell me, Rachael."

Her lips began to tremble, and she stuttered in parts, but told him all that had happened between her and Lloyd Longfellow. Samuel

82

stared, looking straight ahead, and then panted, as if suffocating. Rachael put her hand on his shoulder, to lend comfort, but he recoiled, and got out of the buggy, staggered up to his horse and hugged its neck.

"Samuel," Rachael begged. "Come back so we can talk. I have more to say…"

He lifted his face away from the horse, and by the full moon, Rachael could see tears streaming down his face. "There's more?" he shouted. "More to confess? And I thought I knew you!' At that, he clenched his fists and turned to hit a nearby tree. "I'll kill him. Longfellow," he spewed. Hitting the tree again, he fell to his knees and wept, and shouted things Rachael never imagined could escape his lips.

Another buggy came by and it was Elder Alan. He stopped to try to calm Samuel, but wasn't successful. He told Rachael he'd stay with Samuel while his wife took her home in their buggy. The scene being surreal, Rachael complied.

CHAPTER 8

A Mistake

*C*hristmas preparations were evident throughout Troutville. Many Amish were busy packing to leave to visit relatives or cleaning to receive them. But thankfully, some of her students weren't too busy to help clean up the schoolhouse. Rachael was running late, having tossed and turned most of the night, sleep-deprived, shocked at Samuel's behavior. When she pulled into the schoolyard, she quickly ran to the kindling box, hoping to find a note from him, but there was nothing.

"Teacher, I'm here to help you," Lydia Hostetler said, grinning. "And I brought you a Christmas present."

The love of children. Maybe it's enough for me to teach the rest of my days, Rachael thought. After she hitched her horse to the post, she took the white pastry bag that Lydia held up. "Is it a donut?"

"*Nee.* Something I made for you."

Rachael opened the bag to find a candlestick holder, made of flour and salt dough, painted with water colors. "Lydia, I'll be sure to treasure this always. Maybe put a candle in it and light it every Christmas as a new tradition."

"Teacher, have you been crying?"

"*Ach*, I'm tired," Rachael lied "Didn't sleep well. Keep rubbing my eyes. You go on inside and start taking the pine branches off the window sills. Put them in a pile outside so the birds can use them for shelter."

Lydia glowed and ran into the school. Rachael brought in an armful of kindling, hoping to get a fire started quickly. She usually started with a few sticks but with it being so cold, she lit some paper under a large stack of kindling and then shoved in a log to catch fire.

Several children were taking the branches outside and Rachael got the broom and started to sweep. Candy wrappers, program pamphlets the *kinner* made, Rachael swept into the dust pan and threw it in the fire. The children took buckets of water and started to wash the windows and Rachael, needing to use the outhouse, excused herself, asking the oldest boy to be in charge.

But when she got to the outhouse, the tears wouldn't stop. Knowing no one could hear, she wept aloud, crying out to God in sobs. The absence of her sister during such a time of distress added to her sorrow, and her body jerked as she let the tears flow.

Knowing there were older children in the schoolhouse to watch the little ones, as was their way, she made her way quickly to a grove of pine trees further away from the school to collect herself. To keep the rushing wave of grief over Kate and the rejection of Samuel from swallowing her, she took deep breaths. She thought of Granny Weaver's cozy kitchen. She'd be there in a few days. Rachael stood shivering, but it didn't scare the pair of mourning doves from landing near her. They mated for life; true love... something she would not have on this earth.

She heard screams in the distance and then a popping sound, then others screaming. Rachael darted towards the schoolhouse and soon saw black smoke, billowing up like a mushroom from the school. Lord, no!

"It's a chimney fire," someone yelled.

Rachael ran as if in slow motion, and when within earshot, she yelled, "Run! Everybody out!"

The children ran out of the building as the brisk wind made the fire lick up flames onto one side of the roof. Rachael counted heads, but one was missing. *Lydia!*

Without hesitating, Rachael ran into the schoolhouse.

~*~

Mattie was held tight by Eli and Sadie on either side, keeping her from Rachael's still body that lay on a stretcher. The sirens of fire trucks and ambulances echoed in her heart, the same sounds that chilled her, remembering Kate's accident. "Lord, you can't do this…"

Eli embraced her and stroked her back. "*Mamm*, they said she has a chance."

She has a chance. "That's what they said about Kate."

Eli tried to calm her, but she would not be comforted.

"Look, Lydia is standing up," Sadie gasped. "Praise be."

Mattie stared at little Lydia Hostetler as her *mamm* came to envelop her, her *daed* also.

"How did this all happen?" Mattie blurted.

Arnold, a red-headed sixth grader, was shaking uncontrollably, but turned and said, "Chimney fire. Everyone was out but Lydia. Rachael went in to get her." He burst into tears. "I just stood there. I did nothing!"

One of the many paramedics took Arnold by the shoulders. "Son, you were in shock. You couldn't move."

"But Rachael could!" Mattie shouted. "Wasn't she in shock?"

"Your *dochder* has a strong maternal instinct towards these children," the medic said. "She lifted a roof beam to get to the child." He scratched his chin. "I thought the girl was hers. Most unusual."

Rachael felt called to be a teacher, Mattie thought, *and I will never discourage it again.* Mattie noticed an Amish man running towards Rachael, begging to get through, but the medics and fire crew stopped him. The smoke that still billowed from the schoolhouse made it hard to make out his face, but Mattie was sure it was Samuel. He loves her. *Lord, help my Rachael. Don't take her. I need her. Samuel needs her...*

~*~

Three days later, Rachael awoke lying in a hospital bed, her hands wrapped in bandages and an oxygen tube under her nose. Why couldn't she move? she wondered, panicking. Rachael tried to yell for help, but she could only make a faint, hoarse call. Quickly several people were standing around her, her *mamm, daed*, Eli, Sadie and Samuel. Many started to cry, and fear gripped her again. Why couldn't she move?

Her *mamm* leaned close. "Rachael, so *goot* to hear your voice."

"I... can't...move." She felt like mud was stuck in her throat.

"Doctor said it's smoke inhalation." Mattie readjusted the tubes that lay under Rachael's nostrils. "Keep breathing, nice and deep."

Her *daed* leaned near. "You're tired, too, because it must've taken a lot of energy to save someone's life."

"Lydia's okay?"

"*Ya*, Lydia's in the hospital, too," Eli said. "*Yinz* needed oxygen."

"My hands?" Rachael asked as fear twisted into her heart. Did she still have all ten fingers?

Sadie started to cry, but wiped her face. "Is it painful?"

Rachael wanted to scream yes, but couldn't. "Yes," she croaked, attempting a smile. "All ten there?"

Sadie shook her head. "*Ya*, You didn't lose a finger."

Samuel stood at the bottom of her bed, his eyes sunken and dark. Thoughts of him leaving her in the buggy, pounding a tree, screaming with disgust about her sin settled into her mind. By his expression, he didn't forgive her. Did he think she deserved fire? Hell fire? She wanted him to leave, stop staring. She looked over at her *mamm*. "Tell Samuel to leave."

Mattie frowned. "Why?"

Rachael blinked her eyes rapidly, trying to stay awake, but surrendered to sleep when she had no more strength.

~*~

Rachael opened her eyes as pain darted through her hand, out to her fingertips. Cringing, she wanted to push away the nurse who routinely changed the bandages on her hands. But after getting her bearings, she realized she was home, in Eli's old bedroom, across from her parents.

"So sorry, Rachael," Mattie said softly as if not to wake her. "Need to clean the burns."

Rachael bit her lip and held her breath as her *mamm* unwrapped the bandage off of her left hand and forearm.

"*Ach*, this is healing nicely," Mattie said. "You've come so far in two weeks."

"Ouch," Rachael let out in a moan. "A nightmare."

"You saved Lydia's life, you know, and I'll never doubt your calling again."

"My calling?"

"To teach."

After dressing and wrapping one hand, Mattie got up and brought a vase full of red roses over for her *dochder* to see. "These are from Granny. Delivered in a fancy van with flowers painted on it."

Rachael bit back unbidden tears. "Roses, they helped Granny heal…" She looked at her bandaged hands. *"Mamm*, will my hands ever heal?"

Mattie placed the flowers on the nightstand and sat in a chair near the bed. "Rachael, it may take time, but the doctors believe in a full recovery."

Rachael forced a smile. "Can't bake pies and whatnot with you if my hands can't work."

"Ach," Mattie said with a gasp. "Rachael, you could have died. I'm so thankful you're here. And my heart swells with pride, of a *goot* kind, to have a *dochder* who would risk her life for another. Little Lydia is still recovering, like you, but expected to be right as rain again." She touched Rachael's cheek. "Are you up for visitors?"

"Who?"

"Well, Samuel. He's been like an angel sent from heaven to us. Chopping wood, helping in the barn, helping change your bandages to give me a break."

Rachael gawked. "He was in here?"

"*Ya*, but you were asleep. Pain medicine's awfully strong. He's downstairs."

Rachael shook her head. "*Mamm*, he feels guilty."

"Guilty? For what?"

Rachael breathed deeply. "I told him about Lloyd and he knows how horrible he acted when I told him, stopping the buggy, pounding anything in front of him."

"I didn't know…"

"Well, I got no sleep the night before the accident, rattled to my core. So sleep-deprived, I overloaded the woodstove at school, something I've never done."

Mattie leaned forward. "We all have feet of clay, Rachael, you know that. He loves you, or he wouldn't have been so hurt." Mattie stood up and arched her back. "It's January sixth, Old Christmas and I'd like to have a day off for reflection. Samuel wants to tend to you, so he's coming up."

Rachael wanted to beg her *mamm* to stay, but couldn't. She'd been by her side through this whole ordeal, sleeping in a chair next to her. "*Mamm, danki* for everything. You take a break."

Mattie touched her face again. "I'll bring up some pie later on."

"We fast on Old Christmas, *Mamm*."

"You need your strength."

Rachael nodded and watched her *mamm* leave the bedroom. *Lord, bless her. And help me face Samuel…*

She heard footsteps ascending and fear gripped her, so she closed her eyes. Maybe he'd think she was sleeping. Supposedly she slept while he changed bandages before. Then she thought of what Granny said about hiding. 'A seed is dead as it hides under the earth. But let the water of God's love and others bring it back to life.' Rachael opened her eyes to greet Samuel. "Hello."

Samuel's chin quivered and he quickly turned, and then his shoulders shook and sobs echoed around the room.

Rachael's brow knit together. *No one deserved this amount of guilt.* "Samuel," she yelled above the din. "It's not your fault."

Taking a handkerchief from his pocket, he cleaned up his face, now dotted with red blotches. "I can't stand to see you in such pain." He made his way to the chair next to her bed. "I did feel responsible for the fire. I upset you the night before, but it was an accident. Someone put kiln dried wood in the firebox. Most likely scraps from the furniture store got mixed in when someone filled it. You know using wood dried in a kiln is dangerous."

Rachael gasped. "*Ya*, I do."

"Some had stain on it, too. Chemicals mixed in with dry wood caused the chimney fire." He let out a gasp of air. "It was an accident."

Rachael tore her eyes away from Samuel's. She was relieved that there was an explanation for the cause of the fire. *An accident?*

Samuel shifted in the chair and cleared his throat. Rachael, I became a crazy man, right in front of you. I'm so ashamed. Elder Alan helped, and we ended up talking half the night. And I realize something…"

"What?"

"Well, Jeb Weaver's letters didn't make sense until now. I wrote to him about you, telling him I was in love. His advice was to confess my own sins. I think he could read between the lines that I had a short fuse. Well, he was right. I cursed God, and swore, using vulgar words."

Rachael put a bandaged hand to his cheek, although it was painful. "We all have feet of clay, able to fall, Samuel. And I think Jeb and

Granny talk a lot about confession because they see the benefit. We stumble daily, *ya?*"

He touched her hand tenderly. "I didn't stumble, I sinned. I blasphemed the name of God because I was in a rage." He pursed his lips as perspiration beaded over his forehead. "I wanted to kill Lloyd, too. In my heart, I wanted him dead, so I sinned as if I did the real thing."

Pity filled Rachael. It was obvious Samuel had a contrite heart, one that cut him to his core, due to sin. "Samuel, have you asked God to forgive you?"

He nodded. "Every day. I ask it every day."

"Though your sins be as red as scarlet, He will make you as white as snow. That's what Granny taught me. If I can forgive myself, you can forgive yourself."

As they sat in silence, holding hands, Rachael's mind whirled to the fact that it was no one's fault that the fire started. Could it be that it was no one's fault that Kate died? It could have been unknown factors, things no one would know until they reached Glory.

She met Samuel's handsome eyes. "Don't go down the same path of guilt that I went down. Let's forgive ourselves and each other and move on with our future."

Samuel leaned down and kissed her on the cheek. "Our future? Together?"

"*Ya*, Samuel, I love you," she whispered.

"What did you say?" He shook his head in disbelief. "I don't think I heard you clearly."

Rachael laughed. "*Ach*, Samuel, you heard me. I love you."

Samuel stood up and twirled around comically. "Finally! Does that mean you'll marry me?"

Rachael felt joy deep within, deep healing. "*Ya*, I'll marry you next November."

"Why wait until November? How about February? You always wanted a winter wedding."

She looked down at her bandaged hands. "Will they be healed by then?"

He sat next to her and kissed her again. "We'll talk to the doctor." He kissed her nose. "*Ach*, Rachael, I knew you were the one for me. Promise me you won't hide things again. We'll face our faults together. Pray for each other…"

Rachael never had a heart so full, so free. What a team they would make, helping each other through life, not keeping themselves shut out from healing. Healing that started with the love of God and the love of his people.

Rachael looked over at the vase full of red roses. Thank you, Lord, for my pen pal.

CHAPTER 9

A Healing

*T*he next day, Mattie ran into the room, eyes streaming with tears. "She talked about heaven." She held up a crimson colored journal, and then held it to her heart. "I found it, hidden beneath that old one-foot-long floorboard your *daed* fixed years ago....*Ach*, she asked that her bed be moved over it, remember?"

"Kate's journal?" Rachael froze, feeling this was too good to take in. Everything was left untouched on Kate's side, even the quilt and hope chest stayed where they were. It helped her feel that Kate was still in the room. But she'd mopped the floor, moving the furniture. "I don't understand. I cleaned her side."

"Kate was a sly one, for sure and for certain. And a *goot* carpenter," Mattie laughed. "She lifted up the floorboard, put a hinge on one side and used the space to hide her journal. I was scrubbing the floor on my hands and knees and found it."

Mattie, out of breath, plunked herself in the chair next to Rachael's bed. "*Ach*, the guilt I've carried over my dear Kate's death when all along it was Kate's prayer, desire."

"*Mamm*," Rachael gasped. "She wanted to die?"

Mattie cocked her head back. "*Nee*. She couldn't wait to see Jesus face to face. Listen to her last entry:

"When I look up at the crystal clear sky, I yearn for home. A real home. Not a home made of wood, but my eternal home. Seems like all the girls ever talk about is marriage, but I don't. My one desire is to see you, Jesus, face to face. You seem ever so near. In Song of Solomon you say, Come away my beloved. That's what I want more than anything. To be with You. If I told this to anyone, they'd think I was odd. But these are my feelings safely tucked in my journal."

Tears now overtook Rachael. *Kate, you did long for heaven more than anyone, mentioning it so much. Did God answer your prayer? Ach, I'll be with you someday, knowing I'm forgiven and have that blessed hope of heaven.*

~*~

A month later, Rachael's bandages were off, although some of the scarring would be permanent. Her left hand displayed discoloration the most, but she was thankful that she didn't lose any mobility or coordination. She offered to help peel two-hundred pounds of potatoes the day before her wedding, but the womenfolk feared it would pain her. So she was given the 'chore' of icing her wedding cake, a three tiered white cake she and her *mamm* labored over. Now it just needed assembled and iced.

Taking a break, Rachael sipped tea with her *mamm*, and looked outside. The February sun was glistening on the snowy hills of Troutville, covering up the mud that a January thaw left behind. "*Mamm*," Rachael said softly. "Are you missing Kate? Her not being here tomorrow?"

Mattie sipped her tea. "*Ya*, I do. How about you?"

Rachael knew her sister would have been her attendant, sitting at the traditional *Eck* table tucked away in the corner of the house. She'd have the same light blue colored dress as hers, and they would have chattered as they stitched their new dresses. "*Ya, Mamm*, I'll miss her, but not in the way I used to."

"Oh?" Mattie's eyebrows furrowed.

"I see Kate in heaven, looking down on us all. My guilt is gone, and like Granny says, guilt blinds us."

Mattie reached for Rachael's hand. "I know what you mean. My guilt is gone, too, and I see glimpses of heaven all around me. We get a little taste here, but Kate's enjoying it al."

Rachael noticed her *mamm's* hands were now warm, not perpetually cold, even in summer. Her nerves had calmed. "Thank God for Granny. Her letters to us were ever so helpful."

Mattie gulped. "*Ach*, I forgot. She sent a card."

"Really?" Rachael beamed.

Mattie went over to her basket that hung on the wall. "Here you go."

Rachael tore it open and saw a card, red embossed roses along the edges. It was blank inside, except for a note from Granny. Rachael read it aloud:

My Dear Rachael,

Joy can't express the feeling I have today. To know that you'll be wedding Samuel this Thursday makes my heart glad. Ever so sorry we can't make the wedding, but Jeb's down with a bad cold and truth be told, I have the sniffles, too.

I like to give gifts, but yours isn't ready. Why you may ask? Well, it's because it isn't born yet. Come spring, I'm giving you two lambs, the pick of the litter. I know Samuel has forty acres, and they'll have plenty of pasture. I just ask that you share the wool with your mamm. She'll need lots of yarn for her new business. Will you help her with it?

Please come down to Smicksburg soon.

Love,

Granny Weaver.

Rachael held one hand to a cheek. "Two lambs? *Ach*, so generous."

"*Ya*," Mattie quipped.

"*Mamm*," Rachael said, "I'll do all she says."

"You already have. Rachael, you took correction and guidance like no other."

Rachael grinned. "I don't mean her advice; I mean giving you wool from my sheep, and helping you with your business."

Mattie went over to Rachael, leaned down and hugged her from behind. "*Danki*. Will your hands hurt? Will you be able to knit?"

Rachael put her hands on her *mamm's*. "They're scarred, but fine."

Mattie kissed the top of Rachael's prayer *kapp*. "I'm so glad to get my Rachael back."

Rachael relished in her *mamm's* love. Shame made her hide from these tender moments, but no more. And tomorrow, on her wedding day, Samuel would look at her with steadfast love that cast out guilt. As destructive as guilt was, love was stronger, cleansing her soul.

DISCUSSION GUIDE WITH DR. MARYANN

I thought I would start out by introducing myself to you. Karen and I have been great friends for years, and seeing the need for ministry, she asked me to write this guide. I'm a Christian counselor who ministers to those dealing with pain, betrayal, confusion and crises.

Karen says, "I'll give the characters problems and you can fix them, so my readers can be helped." This is how our collaboration started. Now we both know that it is easy to fix the problems of fictitious characters, but fixing real life can be a challenge. That is why she has asked me to write a guide to help individuals or small groups work through the very real struggles of real life.

A Timely Story

I find the writing of *Rachael's Confession* very timely. In a society in which any of us can find a thousand ways to sin and just as many bad decisions to fix it, we are in desperate need of *clarity*. What I mean is, we need clear understanding of the path that has lead us into sin and we need to seek God's path to lead us out - to freedom.

How This Guide Works

I thought I would frame this guide through a series of questions and in answering them we can more clearly see Rachel's dilemma and how it is solved in a godly way. More importantly, we can use this same model for ourselves. It doesn't matter whether the trouble is an attitude, thought, action or words. It is always in our own best interest to take God's way out.

I believe there can be two helpful uses for this section. The first is as a personal devotional. This way you can have time to do your own personal assessment as to where you are with God; especially if you are feeling distant from God or struggling with past issues. The second use is as a small group discussion; maybe even an accountability group where you trust others and they trust you. In this way you can bare one another's burdens. *Carry each other's burdens, and in this way fulfill the law of Christ. Galatians 6:2*

Where does all the trouble begin?

Granny Weaver asked this question. She knew what Rachel had done didn't occur without a cause. Somewhere in Rachel's pretzel-twisted logic was an issue - a thought - a line of thinking that left her vulnerable to being seduced. Lloyd, making himself sympathetic, positioned himself to pry into Rachel's emotions and her thinking; then distort the beliefs she had taken for granted as truth. All this left her unprepared to rebut his words or his advances.

This unpreparedness allowed Lloyd to redefine her beliefs with the number one lie--God is withholding good. In Genesis, the first book of the Bible, in only the third chapter we see Adam and Eve in a garden of perfection with only one (that's right, one) rule. "You must not eat of the tree of the knowledge of good and evil or you will die." A slithering snake turns and twists God's command, "You surely will not die." And then makes a promise.

"You can be like God knowing good from evil." And it seems we have been falling for that lie and that promise ever since.

This, of course, leads to an entitlement mentality that inevitably questions the goodness of God. Think about it, have we ever complained to God, "Why can't I have...." or accuse God with, "Why did you make this happen?" I'm not speaking of the honest questions that are seeking wisdom and understanding. I'm talking about the questions that really are thinly veiled demands that God should give us what we want because we want it; or that God made a mistake for allowing circumstances in our lives we deem unacceptable. This is the entitled mentality of which I am referring.

At Eli's wedding you see Lloyd up to his games again, but this time Rachel has already experienced the pain of disobedience and the familiar lies of the enemy; lies now embedded more deeply in shame and further unworthiness. She no longer found the "apple" so appealing. Look again at the twisting of truth:

But isn't love from God? You told me that.

Then the deceiving promise:

Rachel, there's nothing wrong with showing love...

Same old devil, same old lies!

Some things to think about...

What areas of your life are vulnerable to the seduction of the enemy's promise? (relationships, financial matters, past hurt, etc.)

*Are you prepared to deal with the temptation that God is holding back good **and** that you are entitled to what you desire?*

What would it take to be prepared to properly handle that kind of temptation?

Wait, there's more!

Later, as Rachel confesses to the bishop and elders, "I allowed him to lure me in."; Bishop John urges Rachel, "Why Rachel? Think back as to why?" Now here in her response, she reveals her deeper vulnerability. "I remember thinking *no one* could be happy with a girl like me ... I'm not pretty enough." Wow! What Rachel (and many of us) was not realizing is that she had sold everyone short. Basically she was saying, "*Every* man and even *God* himself is so superficial that they would not want or love anyone without surface beauty."

Now I don't think Rachel would ever consciously say that or even think that. Yet, that is the implication of her words. It is what became branded on her identity. This is what we intentionally need to be aware.

How wonderful that Rachel had such godly people in her life who took the command in Galatians 6:1 seriously. "Brothers, if someone is caught in a sin, you who are spiritual should restore him gently." They did just that.

Some things to think about…

How do you brand yourselves? What identifying words do you use?
(ugly, uncoordinated, untalented, useless, stupid)

What messages do you tell yourself about yourself?
(I'm not smart enough, no one would miss me, I would only fail if I tried)

What do these messages imply? How do they direct the choices you make?

Are they true? (Don't skip this! Answer this question for every message.)

Do they speak truth about God? You may have to do some serious studying in God's word to answer this.

What is the difference between guilt and conviction?

Guilt is a deadly emotion, one not created by God. Everything God has made is good. But when we decide to live a life apart from God, we're like Adam and Eve in the garden after they ate the forbidden fruit: filled with shame and guilt, hiding from God. This is what Rachael did, and look how destructive it was.

So if we're on the wrong path, how does God correct us? The Bible calls it *conviction*, but in everyday language, is simply means to be convinced of something. God, in His love, *convinces* us of our wrong so we can have a deep relationship with Him. If we hide from God, like Adam and Eve in the Garden of Eden, then we give Satan the opportunity to confuse us with guilty feelings. Guilt is the aftermath of not being in a right relationship with God.

What does this all mean? It means that guilt is *not* for the believer! The guilty are in a helpless and hopeless position; yet, those following God's loving convincing and direction are full of hope. (For a clear path in God's Word on how to come into a trusting relationship with Jesus Christ, please discussion guide.)

Rachel mistook her feelings as guilt which, as a believer, could only come from the enemy of our souls. Innately in guilt is hopelessness. We could see how Rachel was sinking deeper into despair. This is never the purpose of God in the life of the believer. He applies pressure for the purpose of getting us to see the truth of His position. In this, there is freedom – freedom *to* and freedom *from*.

We have freedom *from* the hold of sin and freedom *to* throw off the sins of the past and abstain from that sin again. With all that freedom we now can serve and fellowship with God. This is why I love Galatians 5:1 *It is for freedom that Christ has set us free. Stand firm, then, and do not let yourselves be burdened again by a yoke of slavery."*

Some things to think about...

If you are a believer, do you ever feel stuck in guilt like Rachel? If yes, what is keeping you there?

Is there a lack of confession or repentance?

How do we make matters worse for ourselves?

We've all done it. You know, dig a hole for ourselves and instead of getting out, we just dig deeper. As a counselor I see this all the time. One of the ways we make matters worse is doing what Rachel did for so long. She was drowning in the guilt from the enemy instead of acting on the Holy Spirit who was lovingly nudging her to confess. Though all sin is an offense against God's holiness, there are those sins that have a deeper impact and consequence in our lives. This is where we need the help of trusted believers. Notice I said *trusted.* This cannot be overstated.

We all need those people (and need to become those people) that can maturely and with much grace help move us in the direction of godly obedience. The gossip and the smug need not apply.

I loved how Granny Weaver acknowledged that we all have "feet of clay". This knowledge allowed her to listen with great humility and not set herself above Rachel.

Another way we make matters worse is to believe we are too far gone for God to reach us or love us. If we see God rightly, we see that He has an immeasurable, inexhaustible amount of love for us that lasts forever. This means God never loses or lessens His love for us – ever! Any other thoughts counter to this is a lie. Good news, right?

Meanwhile, here's one more way we complicate things. We can allow ourselves to be "blinded by guilt" and not address the real problem. We become so focused on the feelings of guilt, hopelessness and the message of worthlessness. It envelops us. We can't see the real problem and worse yet, we can't see a way out. This is just one more reason why we need others.

Some things to think about…

Are you telling yourself the truth about yourself, your circumstance, about God?

Do you have a trusted friend, pastor, or counselor to walk with you through the tough times?
If not make this a priority of prayer. Remember, God has an infinite and eternal love for you.

Why is confession not enough?

Confession is a great start. We speak God's view of a situation, idea, attitude or action, but there is more. For example, lying is a sin so we know to stop lying. Lust is a sin so we know to be in right relationship with God we must stop lusting.

We follow the example of the woman caught in adultery and "go and sin no more" as Jesus commanded her. This is called repentance. It is turning in the opposite direction. If we envy, we are to envy no more *and* we are to also rejoice in the joys of others. It is not enough to confess what is wrong; we must then go and do what is right.

Moreover, what we often miss is that not only is sin an offense against God, it harms our relationship with Him and with His people. It separates us from God and from His church. That is why it is so important that Rachel confessed to the bishop and the elders who wisely agreed to keep the confession among themselves. Their purpose was to help free Rachel; not to humiliate her.

The Book of James says, "Therefore confess your sins to each other and pray for each other so that you may be healed."

Some things to think about…

Is there sin in your life that has been hidden and though you no longer commit it, it still weighs heavy on you? This may be what you need to confess to a trusted friend or pastor.

Have you ever experienced the freedom Rachel experienced when she had members of her church supporting her?

What does God really want?

In a word – *restoration*.

Rachel got out of bed every morning, got on her knees and prayed to God to lift the guilt. And yet, it stayed. Was God not listening? Was she not sincere enough? No. God was listening….and waiting. God wasn't the one who heaped on the guilt. Rachel still needed to recognize that. God wanted Rachel to understand the problem with her thinking and she couldn't do that without help.

She saw herself as unworthy because of outward looks; and now, after what she had done, even more so. She devalued her inner person. She did not trust God to do all things; consequently, she was seduced by someone with flattery and the guise of love.

When we don't see God or ourselves rightly (from God's point of view), we have trouble knowing what to do next. Rachel was in this very place; both with her thoughts of herself and her actions after she had allowed herself to be seduced. She had left herself wide open to the deceit of Lloyd and Satan.

God does not bring guilt and condemnation on those that belong to Him. That is what Satan does. Hear this clearly, God does discipline those that belong to Him. He is a father that loves, but He is not playing around. In doing this, He brings us to truth and into an intimate relationship with Himself. Ultimately that is what God wants. He can use our brokenness to do it. Amazing!

Some things to think about...

So, where are you? Do you need to start a relationship with Christ? Or, do you need to renew a lagging relationship with Him?

You may want to highlight in your bible the verses used in this guide that you felt were helpful.

What is it you need to do? Read your bible regularly, find a bible study, and find a trusted friend with which to share life? What about attending church? Studies have shown that couples that attend church faithfully and read their bibles regularly have the absolute lowest divorce rate...hmm

Think about all the things Rachel did that helped her find freedom again. Now, I want you to make your own action plan and receive the joy of life you were created to share with your Creator!

Final Thought

As you find your own freedom, think about Granny Weaver. She was just an ordinary woman walking with her God and living out Galatians 6:9-10:

> *Let us not be weary in well doing, for at the proper time we will reap a harvest if we do not give up. Therefore, as we have opportunity, let us do good to all people, especially to those who belong to the family of believers.*

Are you somebody's Granny Weaver?

Blessings to you!

Maryann

www.maryannroberts.org

How to Know God

God so loved the world, that He gave His only Son, that whoever believes in Him should not perish but have eternal life. *John 3:16*

God so loved the world

God loves you!

"I have loved you with an everlasting love." — Jeremiah 31:3
"Indeed the very hairs of your head are numbered." — Luke 12:7

That He gave His only Son

Who is God's son?

"Jesus answered, 'I am the way and the truth and the life. No one comes to the Father except through me.'" — John 14:6

That whoever believes in Him

Whosoever? Even me?

No matter what you've done, God will receive you into His family. He will change you, so come as you are.

"I am the Lord, the God of all mankind. Is anything too hard for me?" — Jeremiah 32:27

"The Spirit of the Lord will come upon you in power, … and you will be changed into a different person." — 1 Samuel 10:6

Should not perish but have eternal life

Can I have that "blessed hope" of spending eternity with God?

"I write these things to you who believe in the name of Son of God so that you may know that you have eternal life." - 1 John 5:13

To know Jesus, come as you are and humbly admit you're a sinner. A sinner is someone who has missed the target of God's perfect holiness. I think we all qualify to be sinners. Open the door of your heart and let Christ in. He'll cleanse you from all sins. He says he stands at the door of your heart and knocks. Let Him in. Talk to Jesus like a friend…because when you open the door of your heart, you have a friend eager to come inside.

Bless you!

If you have any questions, contact Karen at www.karenannavogel.com

About the Authors

Best-selling author **Karen Anna Vogel** is a trusted *English* friend among Amish in Western PA, and NY. She strives to realistically portray these wonderful people she admires, most stories being based on true stories. Karen writes full-length novels, novellas and short story serials. She hopes readers will learn more about Amish culture and traditions, and realize you don't have to be Amish to live a simple life.

Visit her blog, Amish Crossings, at www.karenannavogel.blogspot.com

Talk to her on Facebook at www.facebook.com/VogelReaders

Or at www.karenannavogel.com

Dr. Maryann Roberts is a nationally licensed pastoral counselor through the National Christian Counselor Association and is board certified in Marriage and Family. She is also an ordained minister of counseling and has been in practice since 2000 helping couples, individuals, teens and at times children to integrate their Christian faith with Christian living within their families and relationships.

Contact her at www.maryannroberts.org

A Special thank you to:
Our editors extraordinaire, Grace Yee and Kara Farnam
Our husbands for having the full time jobs so we can "play" at writing. As always, Jesus, who keeps us knit together in His love. .

Thanks for taking the time to read this story
by Karen Anna Vogel; we hope you enjoyed it.

You may also enjoy other works by Karen Anna Vogel published by Helping
Hands Press www.myhelpinghandspress.org

Amish Knitting Circle Continuing Serial
Amish Knitting Circle 1
Amish Knitting Circle Volume 1 – Beginnings
Amish Knitting Circle Volume 2 – Wedding Season
Amish Knitting Circle Volume 3 – Thanksgiving
Amish Knitting Circle Volume 4 – Snowflakes
Amish Knitting Circle Volume 5 - Christmas Cookies
Amish Knitting Circle Volume 6 - Old Christmas
Amish Knitting Circle Volume 7 - Beauty for Ashes
Amish Knitting Circle Volume 8 - Wings to Fly
Amish Knitting Circle Volume 9 Spun Together
Amish Knitting Circle Volume 10 New Beginnings
Amish Knitting Circle Complete Series (includes Vol. 1-10)

Amish Knitting Circle Series 2
Amish Friends Knitting Circle Volume 1 – A Time to Plant
Amish Friends Knitting Circle Volume 2 – Singing Teakettles
Amish Friends Knitting Circle Volume 3 – Berry Picking
Amish Friends Knitting Circle Volume 4 – Peaches and Cream
Amish Friends Knitting Circle Volume 5 – The Bridge
Amish Friends Knitting Circle Volume 6 – Putting Up
Amish Friends Knitting Circle Volume 7 – Beauty for Ashes
Amish Friends Knitting Circle Volume 8 – Autumn Changes
Amish Friends Knitting Circle Complete Series (includes Vol. 1-8)

Amish Knitting Circle 3
Amish Knit Lit Circle Volume 1: Pride & Prejudice
Amish Knit Lit Circle Volume 2: Little Women
Amish Knit Lit Circle Volume 3: Anne of Green Gables
Amish Knit Lit Circle Volume 4: Dickens of a Tale
Amish Knit Lit Circle Volume 5: Jane Austen's Emma
Amish Knit Lit Circle Volume 6: Black Beauty

Amish Knit Lit Circle Volume 7: Pilgrim's Progress
Amish Knit Lit Circle Volume 8: Secret Garden
Amish Knit Lit Circle: Complete Series (Includes Volumes 1-8)

Full length novels with Helping Hands Press

Knit Together: An Amish Knitting Novel
The Amish Doll: An Amish Knitting Novel

Novellas with Helping Hands Press

Amish Knitting Circle Christmas: Granny & Jeb's Love Story
Christmas Union: Quaker Abolitionist of Chester County, PA